W9-BZW-288

Property of
Bogota Public Library
(201) 488-7185

2/03

MOBY DICK

BASED ON THE NOVEL BY
HERMAN MELVILLE

RETELLING BY
LEW SAYRE SCHWARTZ

ILLUSTRATIONS BY
DICK GIORDANO

HISTORICAL TEXT BY **STEVE URBON**

COLORIST, **DANIEL VOZZO**

Bogota Public Library
375 Larch Avenue
Bogota, NJ 07603

Houghton Mifflin Company Boston 2002

For Roy Crane, the father of the adventure comic,
and Milton Caniff, who still carry the torch of inspiration we will always remember.
—L.S.S. and D.G.

Special thanks to John Costanza, lettering; Frederick M. Kalisz Jr., Mayor of the
City of New Bedford; George Leontire, New Bedford City Solicitor;
The New Bedford City Council; Irwin Marks, Michael Jehle, and Anne Brengle of
The New Bedford Whaling Museum; Arthur Motta, Director of Marketing
and Tourism, City of New Bedford; Pat Bastienne, Graphics Assistant; The Kendall
Whaling Museum; Jay Avila, Spinner Publications; and Gordon H. Wolfe.

Painting on page 4 used with permission of the Board of Trustees of the New Bedford Free Public Library.
Painting on page 47 from the Kendall Museum collection, used with permission of the New Bedford Whaling Museum.

Copyright © 2001 by The City of New Bedford

All rights reserved. For information about permission to reproduce selections from this book, write to
Permissions, Houghton Mifflin Company, 215 Park Avenue South, New York, New York 10003.
First published by the City of New Bedford, Massachusetts.

www.houghtonmifflinbooks.com

Library of Congress Cataloging-in-Publication data is available for this title.
ISBN 0-618-26571-6 (hardcover)
ISBN 0-618-26572-4 (paperback)

Printed in Singapore
TWP 10 9 8 7 6 5 4 3 2 1

CONTENTS

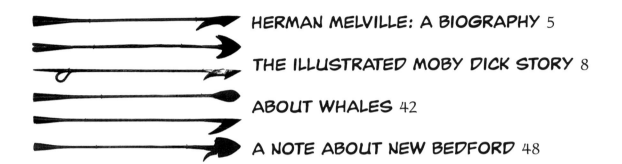

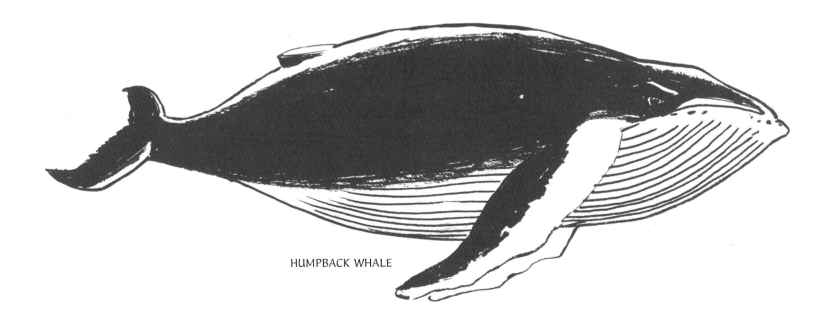

HUMPBACK WHALE

"Built in Mattapoisett, 1840.   Similar to the "Chas W. Morgan", in design, length: 104 ft., 6 in., beam about 27 ft. ⟶ 359 Tons.

Ship, Acushnet, upon which Herman Melville sailed.

The famed author of "Moby Dick", shipped from New Bedford, Dec. 30, 1840, for whaling data.

HERMAN MELVILLE
1819-1891

It was 1819. The United States of America was a very young nation when Herman Melville was born on August 19 of that year. He was the third of eight children (four boys and four girls), and the family lived comfortably in New York City. Herman's father, Allan Melville, had been making a very good living as an importer, arranging for goods to be brought to America from other countries, especially France.

In the years after Herman was born, his father's business began to fail. The family struggled without much money for several years, then moved to upstate New York to start a new business. This time, they tried trading furs. But this venture failed as well, and, two years later, broke, overworked, and tired, Allan Melville died, leaving his young family with no income. Herman's mother, Maria, even though she was from an important family, had no money of her own, and she and the children had to rely on their relatives to help them survive. It was a hard time.

Herman was thirteen and had gone to school for only two years when his father died. Now, to help his family, he took a low-paying job at a bank. By the time he turned eighteen, Herman had had only four years of formal education. But during that time he joined a literary society, a club where books were read and discussed, and he sometimes wrote for the local newspaper. He taught himself by reading everything he could. He then tried teaching elementary school, but it paid him very little, and sometimes he couldn't even collect the money.

Restless and poor, Herman decided to go to sea in the summer of 1839 on a merchant ship bound for Liverpool, England. The trip took four months in each direction. The next summer, he headed west. He followed the Erie Canal, the amazing new waterway that connected the Hudson River in Albany, New York, with Lake Erie. More than 350 miles long, the canal, a man-made river built so that boats could go where they never could before, was at that time the biggest construction project ever attempted in America.

After reaching the end of the canal, Herman headed farther west. He traveled toward the American frontier, toward unexplored lands. His trip took him to the lead mining country in Illinois, where he lived with an uncle. But he still couldn't find work.

So after traveling farther west to the newly explored headwaters of the Mississippi River and then downstream to the frontier town of St. Louis, Missouri, Herman decided to return to New York. There, he tried to get work as a clerk for a lawyer. But those were the days before typewriters, and Herman's handwriting was so bad that no one would hire him.

With no job and not much hope of finding one, Herman did what many young men did in those days: he went to sea once again. This time, in search of adventure, he decided to go whaling. It was dangerous and exciting to catch whales for their precious oil, the finest lamp oil that could be found in the days before electric lights. On Christmas Day in 1840, he signed aboard the new ship *Acushnet*. After attending a Sunday service at the Seamen's Bethel on Johnnycake Hill, Melville sailed out of the busy harbor in New Bedford, Massachusetts, on January 3, 1841.

It was to be a journey of almost four years. The ship first went east to the Azores, then south to Rio de Janeiro in Brazil and around the tip of South America, called Cape Horn. Then it turned north to the Galápagos Islands in the Pacific Ocean. From there the *Acushnet* headed west to the South Pacific islands.

Life on the ship was miserable. The captain was cruel, the crew was uncivilized, and the filth and degradation were awful. On July 9, 1842, Herman and a companion, Richard Tobias Greene, deserted the ship at Nukahiva in the Marquesas Islands.

Now they had a new problem: cannibals! The valley where they landed was inhabited by a tribe—the Typees—known for killing and eating people. Melville and his friend were lucky. Their lives were spared. They were adopted and held as pets, as curiosities, and were well treated. Melville began to appreciate the kindness and skills of people whom most Americans and Europeans thought to be savages.

Melville and his friend escaped after a month with the Typees and soon were able to sign up with an Australian whaleship, the *Lucy Ann*. The ship had stopped at the Marquesas Islands, as many whaling ships did, to take on fresh water and maybe a new crew member or two. Unfortunately, this ship turned out to be even worse than the *Acushnet*. The captain was sick, the first mate was a drunk, and the crew wouldn't take orders.

On September 20, when the ship reached the town of Papeete on the island of Tahiti, Melville refused to go back to sea on it. For this he was put on trial, convicted, and sent to jail. The ship sailed off without him. After it did, Melville was allowed to escape, and with another of his shipmates he sailed to the nearby island of Moorea. There, they lived peacefully and happily for a month as beachcombers. On November 3 of that year they again signed up on another whaling ship, the *Charles and Henry*, which was half a world away from its home port of Nantucket. Once aboard, Herman was assigned the duty of harpooner.

The *Charles and Henry* had a quiet voyage to the Hawaiian port town of Lahaina on the island of Maui. Melville liked it there and decided to stay for a while to work as a store clerk. Later, when he had a chance to return to America aboard a U.S. Navy ship, the frigate *United States*, Herman jumped at the chance to go home. The fighting ship sailed on August 17, 1843, for what was supposed to be a quick trip. But it was more than a year before Herman finally reached Boston in October 1844.

Soon, after shaving off his beard (his older brother told him he would look more Christian without it), Herman made his way back to his family in New York, to tell the stories that would later become the subjects of his many books, short stories, and poems. After all this adventure, Herman Melville was only twenty-five years old.

After he returned to the United States from his voyages, Herman discovered a new talent: storytelling. His sisters and their friends would listen for hours as he told his stories about the

South Pacific, cannibals, and whaling. Many times, Herman would use his imagination to add new events to his stories to make them even more exciting. He would also include things that he had learned about the South Pacific but had not experienced himself. His stories were well received, so he began writing them down and eventually sent them to a publisher.

At the time, not much was known in America about the places that Herman had visited, so when his first book, *Typee: A Peep at Polynesian Life*, was published, people were fascinated. Herman started right away on a second book, *Omoo*, which was much like the first one. Herman's publisher in London, however, began to suspect that not everything in these books was true, as he had been promising Herman's readers. In the nick of time, his friend Richard Tobias Greene, who had deserted the whaleship *Acushnet* with him, came to the rescue by backing up Herman's stories of their adventures together.

By now, Herman Melville was a very popular young writer. He spent many days reading the works of famous authors, and after many months produced his next book, a complicated and confusing work called *Mardi*. The book, not surprisingly, was a failure in the bookstores.

To make up for it to his publisher, Herman went back to telling stories about his own experiences. *Redburn, His First Voyage* was a novel based on Herman's first trip on that merchant ship to Liverpool and back. The book was a success, as was his next, *White-Jacket*, which was a novel based on his experiences aboard the U.S. Navy ship from Hawaii to Boston.

It was now 1850, and Herman told his publisher that at last he was halfway through writing a book about a whaling voyage, based on his trip aboard the *Acushnet*, the book that was to become *Moby Dick*. In the summer of that year, however, Herman was introduced to the famous American author Nathaniel Hawthorne and was so inspired by their long conversations that he took another year to turn his new book into a masterpiece.

When *Moby Dick* was published in 1851, the public and the book critics were not impressed. *Moby Dick* did not sell well, perhaps because people of Melville's time did not appreciate its many meanings. Herman kept writing after that, but his career as a published author was nearly at an end. Eventually he found a job working at the Customs Office in New York, where he remained for twenty years. When he died in late 1891, Herman Melville was a forgotten man.

Three decades or so later, however, scholars began to have another look at his work, especially *Moby Dick*. The book came to be studied and admired across America and around the world, translated into dozens of languages. Today *Moby Dick* is thought to be perhaps the greatest book ever written by an American and one of the greatest ever written in the English language.

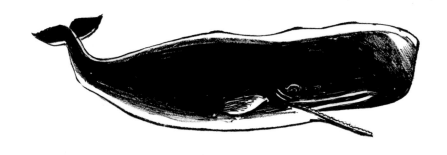

It is on a snowy day in December of 1840 when a young and restless ISHMAEL dreams of going to sea once again. Clearly etched in these daydreams, this time, are visions of great sailing ships, spouting whales, and courageous seamen in small boats battling these monsters of the deep. Now, ISHMAEL stands on a snowy knoll overlooking the beautiful and bustling harbor of the great whaling city of NEW BEDFORD in Massachusetts. The delicious excitement he feels is almost OVERWHELMING!

...SAVAGE?...WHAT'S SO DIFFERENT ABOUT HARPOONERS?

...SAY...THERE'S *NO ONE* HERE!!

HE'LL BE BACK SOON ENOUGH, LADDIE...

HE MUST BE OUT TRYIN' TO PEDDLE THAT PRECIOUS LITTLE SHRUNKEN HEAD HE CARRIES AROUND...

The innkeeper's warnings quickly fade away as Ishmael, overcome with exhaustion, falls into the large and welcoming bed. It takes just seconds for our young adventurer to swiftly sail into a deep and well-earned sleep...Then...SUDDENLY...Ishmael awakens to the presence of someone...OR...*some*thing in the room with him!!!

...There in the dimly lit room looms the forbidding image of Queequeg...harpoon at the ready, poised to sink its sharp head into his shaking body!!

HELP!

...SUDDENLY, the door bursts OPEN

HOLD IT RIGHT THAR QUEEQUEG.

...Y'WOULDN'T WANT T'BE KILLIN' YER' BRAND NEW ROOMMATE NOW, WOULDYA?

And so Queequeg, the "Savage," makes his apologies and soon the two fall into deep conversation about whales and whaling, which lasts into the wee hours...by morning they have become fast friends.

...The next morning they awake early and, as a vow to their newfound friendship, swear to find a berth on a whaleship together. FIRST, however, they attend services at New Bedford's famous Seamen's Bethel, known worldwide as a place to pray for a safe and successful voyage.

FATHER MAPPLE mounts the Bowsprit pulpit, soon mesmerizing the congregation with his incredible rendering of the story of JONAH and the whale ...and how GOD can find you...even at the bottom of the sea!!!

But FATHER MAPPLE's charisma is lost on Queequeg, who promptly falls fast asleep for most of the sermon. On their way out ISHMAEL begins to think that perhaps Queequeg IS a "Savage" after all, but his companionship has become important to him and he puts it out of his mind...So it's off to Nantucket and new adventures!!!

11

...Passage from New Bedford is easily come by on a small packet, the Moss, and the sail, before a brisk wind, is without event. Soon, they drop anchor in the snug, beautiful Nantucket harbor...Now, TO FIND A SHIP!!

A dory comes alongside the packet and it is but a short row to the docks. As they enter the inner harbor they see three whaling vessels apparently taking on huge amounts of supplies. That can only mean ONE THING...they are getting ready to go on a very long journey!!

...SURE LOOKS AS IF WE'RE IN LUCK, QUEEQUEG... WE'D BEST GET ASHORE AND FIND OUT ABOUT A BERTH IN A *HURRY!*

YOU CHOOSE BEST ONE AND QUEEQUEG GET BERTH!

...As if in answer to Ishmael's concerns...at dockside they meet a strange little man who conveys all the information they want...

THE DEVIL-DAM... TH' TIT-BIT, AN' THE PEQUOD ARE ALL READY TO SAIL... TAKE YER' PICK, LADDIES!

THE PEQUOD??

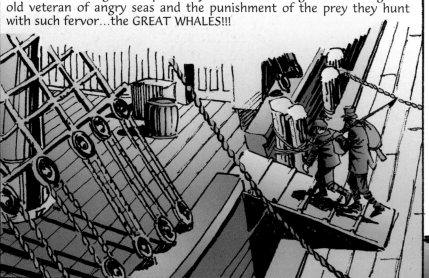

...Before boarding the Pequod they cast an admiring look at this grand old veteran of angry seas and the punishment of the prey they hunt with such fervor...the GREAT WHALES!!!

...Once on board, Captain AHAB is nowhere to be seen, but they are led to one of the owners, who sits in a strange-looking wigwam fashioned from WHALEBONE. The ship's owner quickly takes to Ishmael and signs him on...BUT Queequeg is ANOTHER STORY!!!

...YER' HIRED, LADDIE... BUT, WE'LL BE HAVIN' *NO HEATHENS* ON THIS SHIP!!

...The stranger weaves tale after tale of Ahab's weird and mysterious behavior at sea...Especially alarming is Ahab's haunting manner when there is the smell of fresh whale meat aboard the PEQUOD...

...BEWARE, LADS, YOU AIN'T JUST AGOIN' WHALING...AHAB WANTS ONLY *ONE* WHALE...THE GREAT WHITE THEY CALL *MOBY DICK!*

As they depart, the stranger's bizarre warnings about green moss and St. Elmo's fire follow them.

REMEMBER WELL...SOME SAY AHAB'S A *MADMAN* AN' TH' PEQUOD WILL NEVER SEE NANTUCKET HARBOR EVER AGIN!

...THE NEXT DAY with both crew and supplies all aboard ...the PEQUOD is ready to set sail and make final farewells.

...MAY TH' GOOD LORD LOOK OVER THEE AND BLESS THEE WITH GOOD WEATHER AND A SAFE JOURNEY...

...The wives and children arrive to see their men off to sea...perhaps for several years...perhaps...FOREVER!...Ishmael suddenly spots the Innkeeper from New Bedford in the crowd...AND THEN...

...As if an OMEN...the strange man reappears in the crowd... a prophet of GLOOM?...Maybe, but surely not DOOM!!

...The gangplank is pulled aboard...and the heavy ropes are freed of their captor pilings ...then the cry *"hoist anchor"* is heard as if blasted from a giant trumpet...The crew cheers. The PEQUOD's voyage is NOW under way!!

...Soon the Nantucket shoreline fades well behind, as a cold but welcome wind fills the sails...BUT the captain's bridge remains... *empty*...The strange mystery of Captain Ahab begins AGAIN!!

THE last voice to be heard leaving the harbor cries out, *"We'll sail around the world!!"* and a brisk wind seems to comply...Now Ishmael takes stock of his new shipmates and is struck by the diversity of the PEQUOD's crew... reflecting many ports of call...and many different nations.

...They are East and West Indian, American Indian, African, European, Cape Verdean, Asian, and very brave men the world over...

...AND SO THEY GATHER WITH ONE COMMON PURPOSE, TO HUNT THE GREAT WHALES...AND RISK THEIR LIVES TO LIGHT THE WORLD WITH WHALE OIL.

...Next in order of importance are the Harpooners...

| ...First is the **CHIEF MATE** called by the name of **STARBUCK**... | ...Then there's the **SECOND MATE** called **MR. STUBB**... | ...The **THIRD MATE** is known as **LITTLE FLASK**... | **TASHTEGO** Gay Head Indian | **DAGGOO** African of Gigantic Size | **QUEEQUEG** Ishmael's Shipmate |

...Darkness falls and Ishmael's watch is over. He heads below for some well-earned sleep...BUT...

TAP TAP TAP THUMP THUMP TAP THUMP THUMP TAP TAP THUMP TAP

...before Ishmael's head touches the pillow...a dreaded sound is heard...

...the sound of someone walking the upper deck with a steady...but uneven tread...

'TIS THE DEVIL HIMSELF!!

THE SOUND OF ONE GOOD LEG... ONE *BAD*!

...IT CAN ONLY MEAN ONE THING!

...IT'S AHAB!

...And indeed they were RIGHT!...
The mysterious AHAB has surfaced!!

...And now for the first time since leaving port...days ago...the strange master appears on deck in the light of a full moon. The visit is short-lived, and it is many days before AHAB reappears...Meanwhile the lookout looks not for whales...but for massive icebergs.

...HARD TO PORT! HARD TO PORT... BIG ICE DEAD AHEAD!

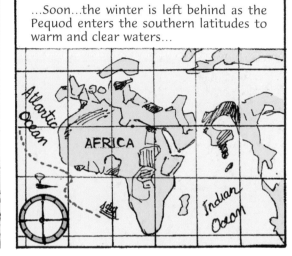

...Soon...the winter is left behind as the Pequod enters the southern latitudes to warm and clear waters...

THE WEATHER WARMS AND THE PEQUOD APPROACHES WHERE WHALES WILL BE FOUND... IT'S NO SURPRISE THAT ONE MORNING CAPTAIN AHAB SUDDENLY APPEARS ON THE AFT DECK IN DAYLIGHT...

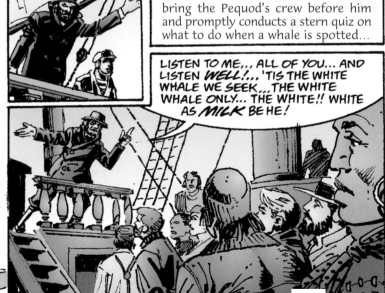

He commands Chief Mate Starbuck to bring the Pequod's crew before him and promptly conducts a stern quiz on what to do when a whale is spotted...

LISTEN TO ME,,, ALL OF YOU... AND LISTEN WELL!...'TIS THE WHITE WHALE WE SEEK...THE WHITE WHALE ONLY... THE WHITE!! WHITE AS MILK BE HE!

...To further demonstrate his resolve, Ahab descends the aft deck...calls for a hammer, and nails a bright Spanish doubloon to the nearest mast...

... AYE, ME HEARTIES... THE FIRST TO SPOT THE GREAT WHITE... WINS TH' GOLD!!

...'TIS DEATH TO THEE MOBY DICK!

...DEATH TO TH' GREAT WHITE!

KILL!

...The crew cheers Ahab, for to them...the doubloon represents a FORTUNE, and sighting Moby Dick will please their captain...BUT, not all hands are quite so happy. After more weeks at sea, Starbuck the chief mate can no longer contain himself, and one day when AHAB confronts him...

STARBUCK FINALLY SPEAKS HIS MIND...

WHAT IS THIS LONG FACE YE WEAR, MR. STARBUCK? ART THOU NOT GAME FOR THE GREAT WHITE?

I'M GAME FOR TH' HUNT, SIRE... BUT I KILL FOR OIL, *NOT* VENGEANCE.

...THIS IS WHAT YE'VE SIGNED ON FOR, MATE!... T'KILL THE BEAST WHAT TOOK ME LEG,... IF WE MUST, TO SEEK THE WIDE WORLD,...UNTIL I'VE MOBY DICK ON THE END OF ME HARPOON!

...AHAB turns and angrily stomps off...

...Before Starbuck can muster a reply...the cry so long waited by the Pequod's crew sounds out LOUD and CLEAR...

THAR SHE BLOWS!!

...THE CREW SCURRIES INTO ACTION

Hearts pound, breaths shorten...and reflexes are set in motion by long experience...They lower the boats into the water in NO TIME. THE CHASE BEGINS!!

...*AWAY THEY GO!!*... EIGHTEEN MEN OFF TO DO BATTLE WITH ONE OF THE MIGHTIEST CREATURES ON THE FACE OF THE *EARTH*...

Their PREY...the lookout has spotted THREE huge sperm whales frolicking in the warm sea waters, a piece of good fortune for the Pequod's crew, since the sperm whale is so highly prized for both the quantity and quality of its oil. The New Bedford owners will be very pleased...The crew sees it as a GOOD OMEN for their voyage...

The SPERM WHALE
A MAMMAL...NOT A FISH

STREAMLINED BODY. 60 FEET IN LENGTH. 90,000 TIMES AS LARGE AS THAT BIG BASS YOU CAUGHT LAST SUMMER.

500 GALLONS OF LIQUID OIL IN TOP OF HEAD.

BRAIN, LARGEST OF ANY MAMMAL

COULD EAT SARDINES BY THE MILLIONS AND STILL BE HUNGRY.

FLUKES, OR TAIL, LIE FLAT.

DIVES HALF MILE, OR MORE, BELOW SURFACE OF OCEAN FOR MEALS, LIKE GIANT SQUID. BLUBBER IS FOOT THICK. SKIN SO THIN IT CAN BE SCRAPED OFF WITH FINGERNAIL.

TEETH ON UNDER JAW ONLY. COULD SWALLOW A HORSE IN ONE GULP.

SOMETIMES TRAVELS IN SCHOOLS OF FOUR OR FIVE HUNDRED. OIL USED IN MAKING SOAP.

CRACK YER BACKBONES! SPLIT YER SIDES! BLAST YE! PULL! ANY MAN AS GITS A'FEARED, I'LL KNOCK 'IM STIFF!

...BUT...they are about to experience the savage ferocity of the sperm whale when under attack...It becomes a KILLER...

...AND THEY LAND ON THE WATER, making a deafening sound...

CRASH!!

...SUDDENLY...out of NOWHERE, all three whales breach the surface...not more than FIFTY feet from their boats...IT'S an INCREDIBLE SIGHT!!

...QUEEQUEG's eyes narrow as they near the surfaced giants... and then he selects his prey...

He looks for the vital spot to thrust home his harpoon...and it's DONE!!

...The sharp blade goes deep and the wounded creature quickly responds...

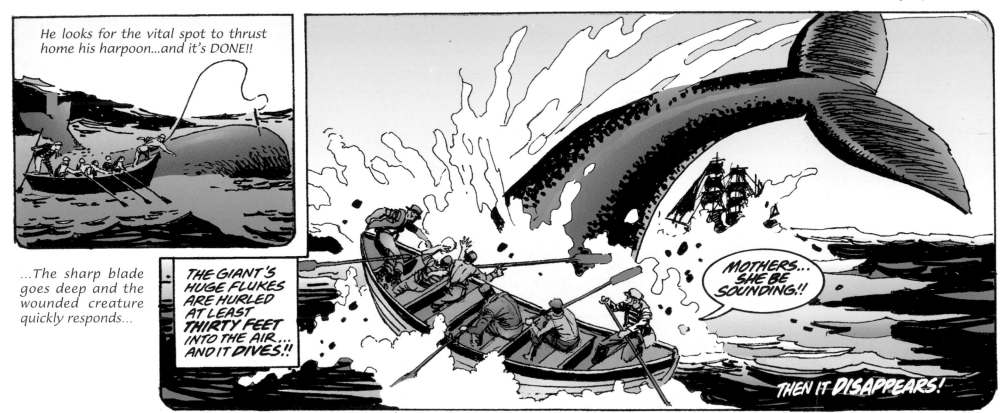

THE GIANT'S HUGE FLUKES ARE HURLED AT LEAST THIRTY FEET INTO THE AIR...AND IT DIVES!!

MOTHERS... SHE BE SOUNDING.!!

THEN IT DISAPPEARS!

...DOWN IT GOES CARRYING THE HARPOON AND ITS LINE INTO THE DEEP...

...And with the power of an express train...the whale runs for its life, carrying the boat miles from the ship.

...HOO-WEE, MAYBE IT WILL TAKE US HOME TO NANTUCKET!

...YE WILL BE LUCKY TO BE ALIVE WHEN THIS *BEAST* BE THROUGH WITH US!!!

...Talk about THRILLS...whalemen called this awesome experience a Nantucket Sleigh Ride.

THE WHALE *SURFACES.*

LET 'IM HA'IT, LET 'IM HA'IT.

...And they narrow their distance as Queequeg prepares to make the DEATH THROW!

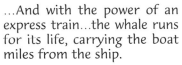

...*MORTALLY WOUNDED, THE GREAT CREATURE ROLLS AND CHURNS THE SEA INTO BLOODY FOAM.... THE WHALE IS DONE AND SO ARE THE WHALERS... NOW THEY MUST SEARCH FOR THE PEQUOD...*

Property of Bogota Public Library (201) 488-7185

21

...Exhausted beyond belief, the crew sits in absolute silence as they watch the gallant giant perform its last rites...Their boat has pulled back to distance them safely from what is now about to occur...

...FIRST is the CRIMSON SPOUT indicating the battle is OVER...

Head held high...the mighty whale spins in a circle...

STARBUCK decides to have all three boats TOW the carcass in the direction the ship was last seen...The SUN is HOT...The whale weighs SIXTY TONS!!

...But now they are miles away from the PEQUOD...

...FIRST is the sickening task of stripping the whale blubber from the carcass...It is just the BEGINNING!!

...With little or no time to recover from their encounter with the whale ...AHAB drives the men without mercy.

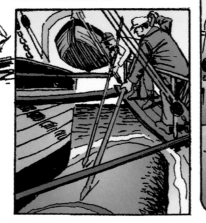

...Just when all hope is lost the PEQUOD appears...The crew CHEERS...but thanks to AHAB it will not be for long!!

...With a SPERM, they first extract the jawbone and teeth...the huge store of oil is bailed from the whale's hollow head...It will bring a fine price in the New Bedford market. The work is backbreaking and AHAB pushes them until they DROP!!

..."OIL FOR THE LAMPS OF AMERICA"...may have been the cry when the Pequod's crew took off to hunt down their first catch...BUT both the chase and AHAB have taken their toll...*Finally* STARBUCK insists the men work in six-hour shifts to relieve their exhaustion...a wise decision and just in time!!...NOW the work continues...

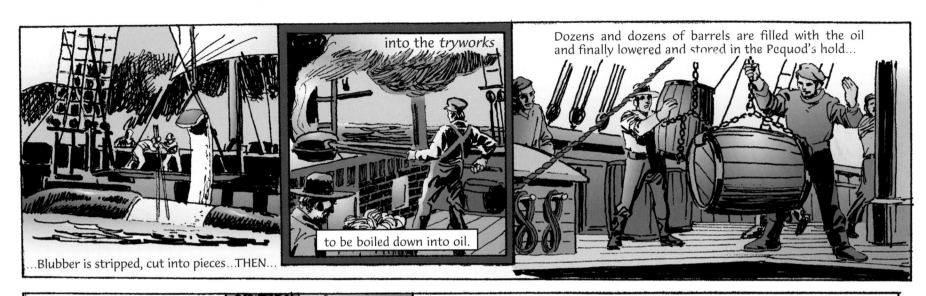

into the *tryworks*

to be boiled down into oil.

...Blubber is stripped, cut into pieces...THEN...

Dozens and dozens of barrels are filled with the oil and finally lowered and stored in the Pequod's hold...

...The bones are thrown overboard and the jaw saved for the huge teeth used to make scrimshaw.

SUDDENLY a cry of joy goes up as Ahab cuts into the whale's digestive tract and finds AMBERGRIS!!!

Rocks of ambergris

AMBERGRIS was once used to make fine perfumes and cost TWICE as much as its weight in GOLD!!...The crew is ecstatic, for not only will the whale oil fill their pockets, but their share of the ambergris will make them very rich men...ONE sperm whale in a thousand is thought to carry the precious rare substance!! The PEQUOD's voyage is now a grand SUCCESS...BUT...

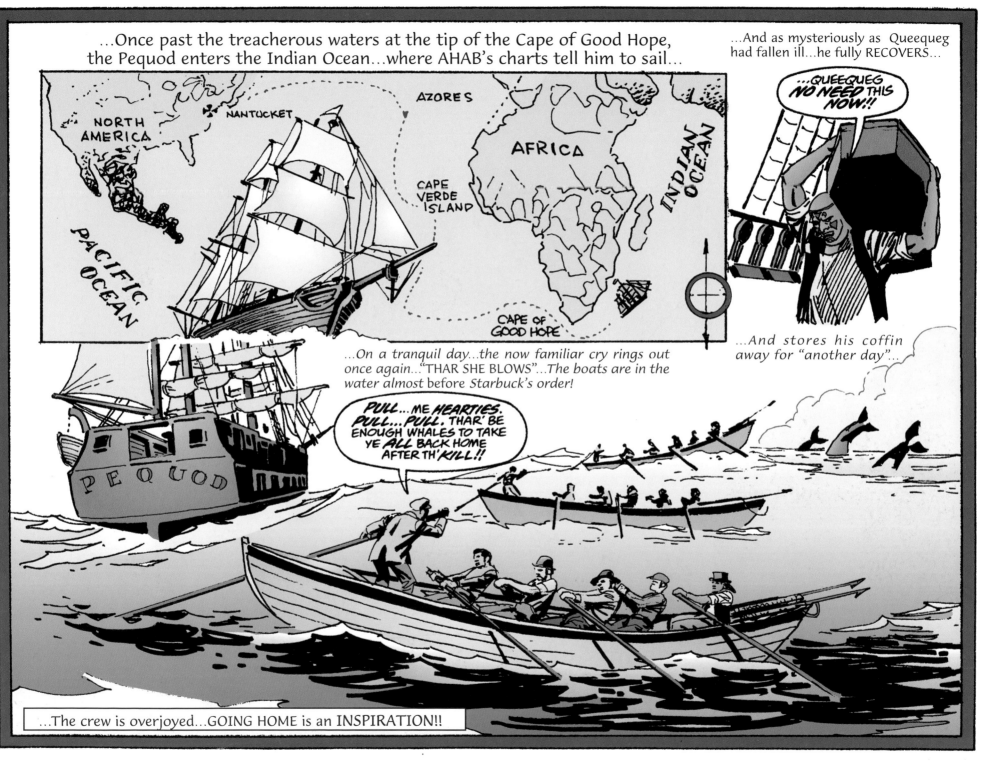

...Once past the treacherous waters at the tip of the Cape of Good Hope, the Pequod enters the Indian Ocean...where AHAB's charts tell him to sail...

...And as mysteriously as Queequeg had fallen ill...he fully RECOVERS...

...QUEEQUEG NO NEED THIS NOW!!

...And stores his coffin away for "another day"...

...On a tranquil day...the now familiar cry rings out once again..."THAR SHE BLOWS"...The boats are in the water almost before Starbuck's order!

PULL...ME HEARTIES. PULL...PULL. THAR' BE ENOUGH WHALES TO TAKE YE ALL BACK HOME AFTER TH'KILL!!

...The crew is overjoyed...GOING HOME is an INSPIRATION!!

WHALES!!...WHALES!!...A whole school OF SPERM WHALES...of every size and shape!! Queequeg selects a gigantic bull and WAITS to makes his move...

...BUT...Tashtego THIRSTS for the KILL and moves TOO QUICKLY...His quarry DIVES...

SUDDENLY...to his surprise, the whale *SURFACES* under the boat...

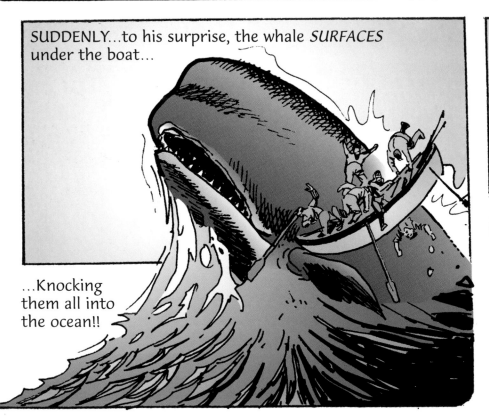

...Knocking them all into the ocean!!

AHOY... PEQUOD!

...Fortunately the boat and most of their equipment are recovered...Since no one was hurt, in short time they are back to the chase...BUT...unknown to the busy whalemen, the PEQUOD has a VISITOR who is about to *SHATTER* their dreams...

...IT is Captain Boomer of the British whaler Albatross... He asks Ahab if he can come aboard the Pequod...

...Ahab doesn't reply. INSTEAD, the dialogue between the two is short with a single purpose.

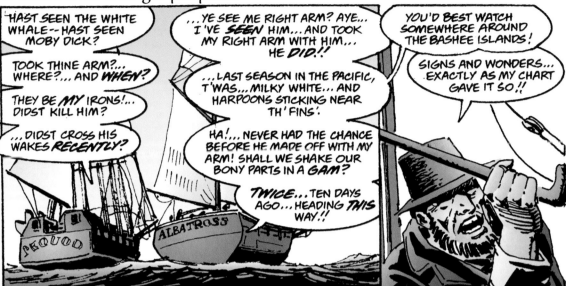

HAST SEEN THE WHITE WHALE -- HAST SEEN MOBY DICK?

TOOK THINE ARM?... WHERE?... AND *WHEN*?

THEY BE *MY* IRONS!... DIDST KILL HIM?

...DIDST CROSS HIS WAKES *RECENTLY*?

...YE SEE ME RIGHT ARM? AYE... I'VE *SEEN* HIM... AND TOOK MY RIGHT ARM WITH HIM... HE *DID.*!!

...LAST SEASON IN THE PACIFIC, T'WAS... MILKY WHITE... AND HARPOONS STICKING NEAR TH' FINS.

HA!... NEVER HAD THE CHANCE BEFORE HE MADE OFF WITH MY ARM! SHALL WE SHAKE OUR BONY PARTS IN A *GAM*?

TWICE... TEN DAYS AGO... HEADING *THIS* WAY!!

YOU'D BEST WATCH SOMEWHERE AROUND THE BASHEE ISLANDS!

SIGNS AND WONDERS... EXACTLY AS MY CHART GAVE IT SO.!!

The crew goes about their business...

Then...the long trek back to the Pequod hauling the huge carcasses behind them...only to hear AHAB's fierce order...

COME ABOARD AT ONCE!

...TO CUT THE BODIES LOOSE and hoist sails...IMMEDIATELY.

...LEAVING THEIR HARD-WON CATCH FAR BEHIND... ITS SAILS FILLED FULL...THE PEQUOD MOVES BRISKLY TOWARD THE PACIFIC AND A RENDEZVOUS WITH MOBY DICK... A VOYAGE OF VENGEANCE THAT BREEDS MUTINY... IN THE HEARTS OF THE CREW...

The crew is angry and DISTRAUGHT

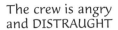

I'LL NOT SEE MY FAMILY AGAIN.

...by Ahab's orders,

THE PEQUOD WILL NEVER RETURN TO NANTUCKET.

And make no secret with each other that

THE CAPTAIN HAS LOST HIS MIND.

SOMETHING must be done...SOON...

BAD MEDICINE TO LEAVE WHALES.

VERY SOON!!

THE PEQUOD ENJOYS BRISK WINDS FOR MANY DAYS...THEN...

GODS NOT LIKE THIS... ISHMAEL!

NOR DO I!

...IS SUDDENLY BECALMED UNDER THE HOT PACIFIC SUN.

...The crew...with little to do, turns its focus on Ahab with growing and intense animosity...

...HEAVEN HELP US! THERE BE GREEN MOSS GROWIN'!

...GREEN MOSS!!...The old man's prophecy was coming TRUE!!...and Ishmael shudders...could it BE???

...But AHAB ignores the omen and instead...orders a new and special harpoon be made for his long-awaited meeting with MOBY DICK...

...AND REMEMBER TH' WHALE I SHALL KILL WITH IT!

...When it is finished he tests the blade and the crew's loyalty by making some of them anoint the razor-sharp blade with their blood...He takes little notice of the very threatening dark clouds descending on them from the east.

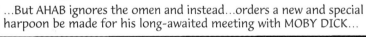

28

ONE DAY THE PEQUOD'S MASTS WILL TURN GREEN ...AND AHAB WILL DIE!

ISHMAEL recalls the prophetic words of the mysterious stranger whom he and Queequeg had first encountered on the docks and the omens of GREEN MOSS on the masts and yardarms that meant trouble for all aboard...He spoke, too, of "ST. ELMO'S FIRE"...THEN Queequeg spots the approaching storm and whispers ONE word..."TYPHOON!!!"

...The Typhoon hits the Pequod with an unbelievable ferocity.

HAVOC ON DECK!!...The storm tears through the Pequod, ripping apart everything in its path...The crew struggles to save the ship...

...And a hapless lookout is plucked from his perch in the crow's nest and thrown into the churning sea...GONE from sight!!!

LORD SAVE US! 'TIS TH' ST. ELMO'S FIRE!!

...As if dissatisfied, the winds batter the Pequod until it begs for MERCY... Then the SECOND omen appears at the top of the masts...

...And the flame descends the mast, flaring up on the very tip of Ahab's blood-smeared harpoon, as if in some evil ceremony...

...The night of TERROR finally subsides...daylight reveals the once-proud ship lying in tatters in a glasslike, tranquil sea ...Fortunately, the Pequod, like most other whaleships, is well prepared to repair the storm damage...But NOT the behavior of AHAB and the succession of evil OMENS...

...Each taking place ONE upon the OTHER leaves the crew in no mood to continue their strange journey...STARBUCK finally speaks up.

...TOO MANY OMENS OF DOOM,,, CAP'N AHAB,,, THE CREW WANTS TO REPAIR TH' SHIP...

And the crew CHEERS his brave stand...

...WE MUST GIVE UP THIS MAD QUEST AND MAKE FAIR WIND HOMEWARD!

...And AHAB's response is PREDICTABLE!!

YOUR OATH!,.. YE SWORE YOUR OATH TO HUNT TH' WHITE WHALE, AN' YE SHALL!

...BEFORE Ahab can truly vent his anger, he is interrupted by a sudden VISITOR...the whaleship Rachel pulls alongside the Pequod...Ahab makes his usual query...a terrible tale unfolds!!

...ANY SIGN OF AN EVIL WHITE WHALE WITH A CROOKED JAW?

...YES,,, BUT I MUST BOARD YOU IMMEDIATELY!!

Before AHAB can agree to the request...a boat has been lowered and the captain rapidly makes for the Pequod...

AHAB's greeting is less than cordial as he watches the RACHEL's captain pull alongside his ship.

...WHAT BE SO GRAVE, CAPTAIN GARDINER, THAT IMPEDES OUR REPAIRS SO WE MAY CONTINUE IN OUR SEARCH FOR TH' GREAT WHITE WHALE?

...YOU MUST HELP US!

AND the story unfolds with terrifying detail.

...Ahab and the crew listen to the captain's story with equal sympathy and HORROR...

... WE HAD LOWERED TO CHASE A SCHOOL OF SPERM... WHEN FROM NOWHERE, TH' WHITE ONE COME UP AN' SNATCHES ONE BOAT...AN' RUNS AWAY WITH IT...CREW AND *ALL*... THE BOAT WITH MY TWELVE-YEAR-OLD *SON!!*

...WE'VE BEEN HUNTING NIGHT AN' DAY... AND TH' BOAT *NEVER CAME BACK!!* IT IS *GONE*... GONE WITH MY YOUNGEST SON!...I'VE COME TO ASK YOU TO HELP US SEARCH FOR HIM AND THE OTHERS... *WE BEG OF YOU*...

AYE, CAPTAIN AHAB!... WE MUST SAVE ALL OF THEM... IF WE CAN.

...To everyone's STUNNED amazement, AHAB REFUSES!!

... IT IS A SORROWFUL TALE CAPTAIN,... BUT WE *CANNOT SPARE* TH' TIME WITH MOBY DICK SO CLOSE AT HAND,... TAKE SOLACE IN THAT WE SHALL SLAY THE MONSTER *FOR* YOU,... MAKE READY AS SOON AS YE CAN, STARBUCK!

BUT... WE *BEG* YOU!

...And so Captain Gardiner returns to his boat, vowing that AHAB's refusal to help find his lost son will bring down a curse upon AHAB and the Pequod's crew...

...And even before the Captain's boat gets back to the Rachel, a flurry of activity is taking place aboard the Pequod, completing repairs on torn sails and broken lines to make the ship seaworthy once more...

...THE LORD WILL SHOW YE TH' *SAME* PITY YOU'VE SHOWN ME SON...*AHAB*!!

STEP LIVELY THERE... GET A MOVE ON LADS!

...MAINS'L AN' LINES ARE READY, MR. STARBUCK!

...AHAB WILL HAVE HIS WAY!!!

...And Queequeg returns carrying the coffin that was prepared for his very *premature* death...

...THE PEQUOD IS SET...AND THE SEARCH FOR THE ELUSIVE MOBY DICK IS UNDER WAY ONCE MORE!!

...Fearful of arousing AHAB's ire, Starbuck takes extra care of even the smallest detail...then discovers...

...WE BE MISSING THE LIFEBUOY THAT WENT DOWN WITH THE LOOKOUT DURIN' TH' STORM...

...ME CAN FIX THAT, MR. STARBUCK!

...YOU SEAL TIGHT! MAKE VERY FINE LIFEBUOY!

...AND INDEED IT WAS!!

PEQUOD

...The Pequod enters the Pacific waters of the Bashees...The wind carries a strangely SWEET SMELL that makes AHAB cry out...

MOBY DICK!...I CAN SMELL THEE!...AND I SHALL HAVE MY HARPOON IN THEE AT LONG LAST!...RIG ME A BASKET *STARBUCK* AND RAISE ME TO THE LOOKOUT!

I SHALL HAVE *FIRST SIGHT* OF TH' BEAST MESELF AND WIN TH' *GOLD DOUBLOON!!*

Ropes are fastened to a basket...and the raging AHAB is hoisted to the crow's nest occupied by a surprised ISHMAEL...

...ISHMAEL surveys all of this with absolute dismay, for the yardarms and the masts seem to be turning GREEN...the PROPHECY of AHAB's death appears to be *playing out!!*

NO SIGNS, CAPTAIN!

CAN YE NOT *SMELL* HIM, LAD?

THEN...as in a SINGLE VOICE comes the cry AHAB has so longed for...

THAR SHE BLOWS!

...And so the sweet words ring out that finally bring joy to AHAB's ears...

...TIS HIM... TH' WHITE WHALE!!

BLOWS! THERE SHE BLOOOWS!

...From the crow's nest AHAB orders the boats into the water and Starbuck to quickly lower him to the deck.

Once on deck, AHAB gets his crew organized and surprises Starbuck with his next order...

MR. STARBUCK... STAY ON BOARD. KEEP TH' SHIP WHILST I GO MYSELF TO MY ENEMY!

...BUT CAPTAIN AHAB?

...HAND ME MY HARPOON STARBUCK!

...AHAB is lowered into the boat.

...AHAB'S BOAT TAKES THE LEAD WITH BOTH ISHMAEL AND QUEEQUEG AT OARS... AND A MILE AWAY... MOBY DICK AWAITS.

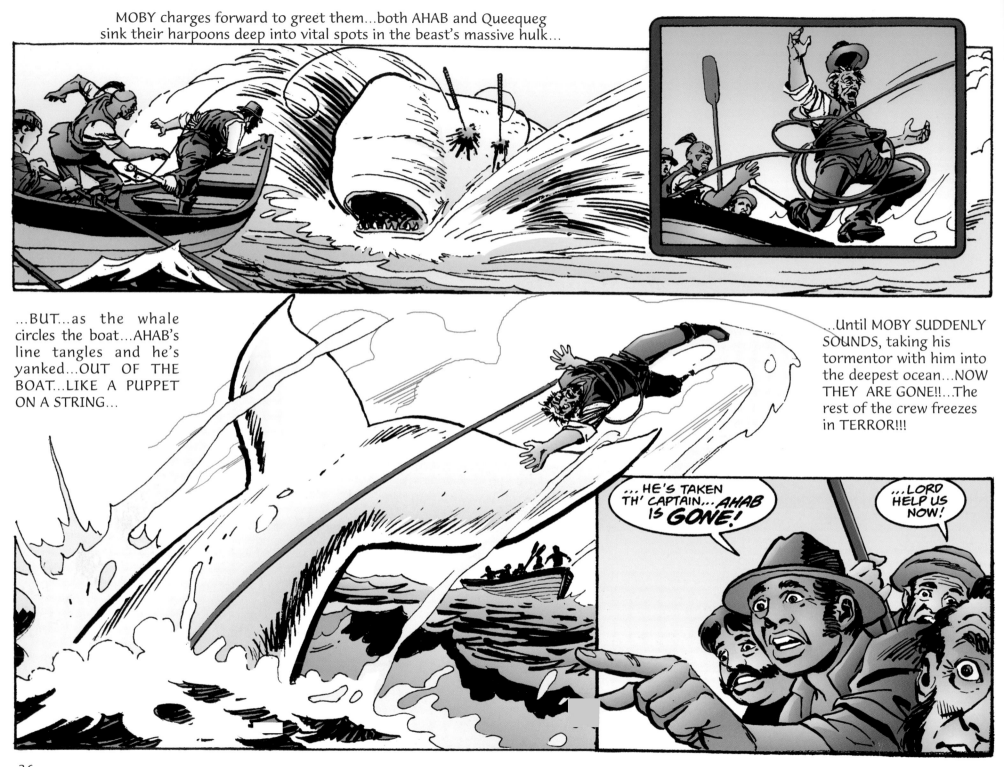

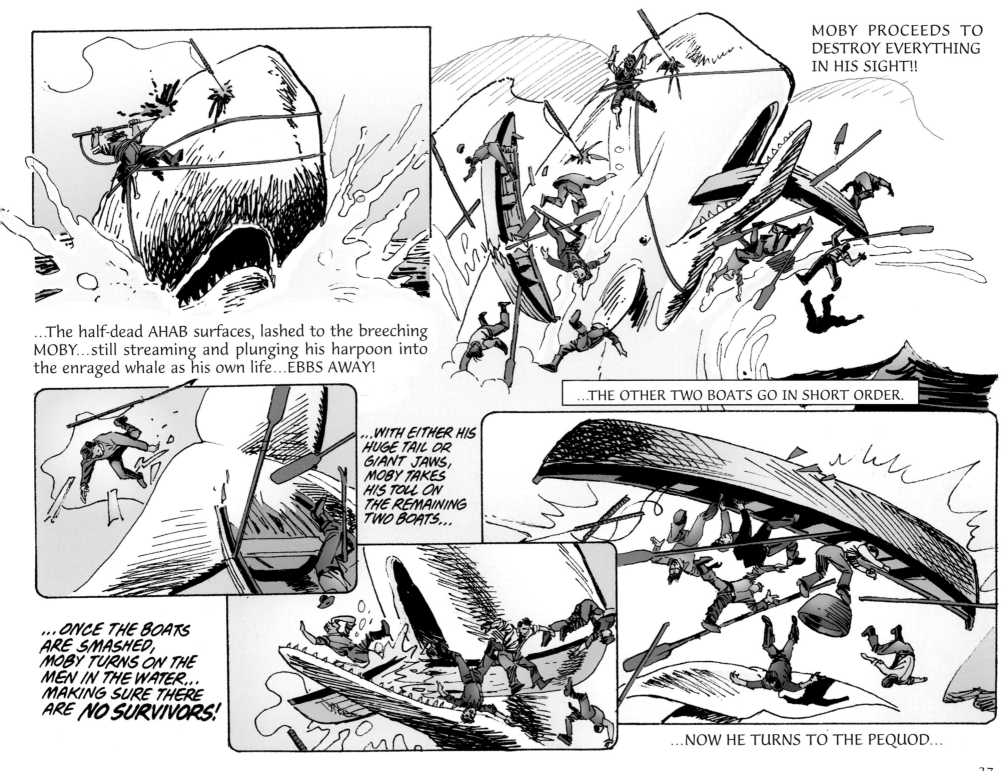

MOBY PROCEEDS TO DESTROY EVERYTHING IN HIS SIGHT!!

...The half-dead AHAB surfaces, lashed to the breeching MOBY...still streaming and plunging his harpoon into the enraged whale as his own life...EBBS AWAY!

...THE OTHER TWO BOATS GO IN SHORT ORDER.

...WITH EITHER HIS HUGE TAIL OR GIANT JAWS, MOBY TAKES HIS TOLL ON THE REMAINING TWO BOATS...

...ONCE THE BOATS ARE SMASHED, MOBY TURNS ON THE MEN IN THE WATER... MAKING SURE THERE ARE **NO SURVIVORS!**

...NOW HE TURNS TO THE PEQUOD...

...As if dissatisfied with the carnage, the huge whale sets his sights on his NEXT VICTIM...

...HYPNOTIZED with fear and utter disbelief...the remaining crew aboard the Pequod watch while the maddened monster bears down on them, determined to seal THEIR fate as he has the OTHERS'! There is no way to outrun or avoid what seems to be INEVITABLE!!

Throughout generations of history, whalemen have recounted unbelievable tales of maddened gargantuan whales turning on their tormentors by battering their boats, then using their massive girth to stave in even the strongest, most noble whaleships...and this was *JUST SUCH A DAY!!*

...A day when vengeful Captain AHAB dies seeking retribution for the leg MOBY DICK took from him so many years ago...NOW... they meet ONCE AGAIN...to become part of one of the great legends of an unrelenting sea and what mysteries lie beneath its surface. ...Unfortunately, the remaining crew aboard the Pequod will soon become part of that story, as MOBY DICK wreaks his anger upon THEM!!

The Pequod slides quickly and majestically into the whirling foam...There appear to be NO SURVIVORS of MOBY's wrath...

SUDDENLY out of nowhere...a half-drowned ISHMAEL surfaces...exhausted...out of breath...THEN...as if an omen he was *meant to survive*...Queequeg's former coffin pops out of the water just a few feet away!

...ISHMAEL barely manages to climb on this unholy life preserver...Night envelops him and he hangs on grimly, fearing sleep that he so desperately needs...It takes an entire lifetime for daylight to finally break...

BLUE WHALE

ABOUT WHALES

Whales are magnificent animals—intelligent, sometimes huge, warm-blooded mammals that spend their entire lives in the ocean. It is hard to imagine, but in Herman Melville's day no one really knew what the largest whales looked like. They were so large that one could not be brought aboard the deck of a ship, and so whalers and scientists had little knowledge of all the varieties of whales and how they live.

Because of this lack of a good picture of the whale, Melville called them "unpainted to the last." Not knowing much about these enormous creatures, people often called them dragons or sea monsters and spun legends about them, though most people believed they were some sort of fish.

Over time, we have come to understand that whales breathe air with lungs rather than filter air from water with gills as fish do. Whales also nurse their young with mother's milk, much the same as land-based mammals. Whales' great tails, too, set them apart from fish: the flukes of a whale's tail move up and down rather than from side to side. And when they exhale through their blowholes, the spout can be seen for miles at sea.

Before man came to hunt them with ships, whales swam by the hundreds of thousands in all the oceans of the world. There are far fewer today, but since most of the world's whaling has ended, the numbers of many whale species have started to increase.

WHALE TRAVEL

Large and powerful, these strong swimmers with enormous tails often migrate thousands of miles between seasons. Whales usually use individual routes, which allowed whalers to track them from year to year and hunt them more efficiently.

Whales travel in groups called pods, which at one time, before commercial whaling, could easily number in the hundreds. Sperm whales such as Moby Dick usually separated by gender, with the smaller females—"cows"—sometimes joined by one or two males. Moby Dick, it appears, traveled alone, as older "bull" whales sometimes do. Whales dive deep and remain submerged for long periods of time. Large sperm whales routinely dive down to 800 meters and have been recorded as deep as 3,000 meters. On one breath of air, whales can remain submerged for ninety minutes or more.

Whales feed in oceans far to the north and south during the warmer months and then move toward the warm waters of the equator to breed during the colder seasons. Young whales need warmer water because they have not yet fully developed the thick layers of blubber that insulate them from the cold. These migrations can be very long; the gray whales in the northern Pacific Ocean travel 5,000 miles twice each year, from their feeding grounds near Alaska to their calving grounds near Baja California.

WHAT WHALES EAT

Most types of whales feed on small, shrimplike creatures called krill. Whales, which can eat a ton and a half of food in a day, take in large mouthfuls of water and then press the water back out through the slats, or baleen, in their mouths, trapping their food.

Moby Dick was a sperm whale. Sperm whales are meat-eaters, carnivores, with huge teeth and terrifying jaws. They usually eat squid, as well as many hundreds of pounds of fish a day.

WHALE INTELLIGENCE

Whales have the largest brains in the animal kingdom, and we are only beginning to learn about how they navigate the oceans and communicate with one another. In the deep, dark ocean, reflected sound replaces light as a tool for finding the way. Sperm whales make very low and very loud sounds—the loudest sounds of any creature—in order to hear the reflections and know where they are going. Whales also "sing" long and elaborate songs to identify themselves and one another during mating season, and to communicate danger.

ALL ABOUT WHALING

People hunted whales for hundreds of years before America was a country.

Native Americans were the first to take whales that had been beached on the shores of New England and nearby Long Island and carve them up for their meat, their bones, and their blubber. When America was an English colony, Indians didn't have ocean-going boats of their own, but they joined the English settlers in their boats and hunted the whales offshore. In time, dozens of wooden lookout towers were built along the coast. Larger and larger boats made it possible to go farther out to sea for still more—and larger—whales.

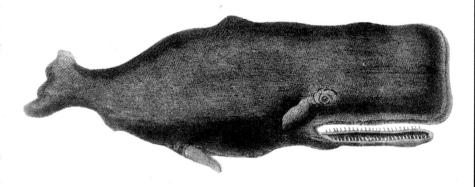

For a century, the island of Nantucket was a busy whaling port because it is twenty miles out to sea, nearer to the whales' migration routes and feeding grounds. As the whaling ships grew larger, however, they could no longer enter the shallow Nantucket harbor. Starting in 1750, New Bedford became a larger whaling port because of its deep harbor. And because New Bedford was not an island, shipping whale oil and whalebone to market was much easier and more profitable. New Bedford was to become known as the Whaling Capital of the World in the 1800s. By 1857, 329 whaling ships called New Bedford their home port, more than half of the whaleships in the country. The famous New Bedford whalers traveled to every ocean, on voyages that lasted for years.

These were the days before electricity, before anyone knew that "rock oil" from the ground could be made into kerosene to light the lamps. Whale oil was used in lamps almost everywhere, and New Bedford's city motto became *"Lucem Diffundo,"* which is Latin for "I spread the light."

Whaling was dangerous. A prized sperm whale like Moby Dick could be a killer. Sperm whales feed not on shrimp or krill but on squid, often giant squid that live near the ocean bottom and are big enough to attack a sperm whale or a whaleship. A sperm whale's high, hard forehead could also become a battering ram, smashing the hull of a whaleship like the *Pequod*.

Whaleships were not like other ships. They didn't go from port to port, carrying cargo and passengers. Instead, they spent months, often years, at sea, carrying everything that the crew would need to live and work for so long. All the clothing, all the food, all the tools—everything for a very long voyage was carried on board. The ships were strong and slow, and except for the captain's quarters they were dark, crowded, and foul-smelling places to live.

All the ships carried whaleboats. These were lowered into the sea and rowed, and sometimes sailed, to catch whales that were spotted by the men at the masthead, on top of the ship's towering masts.

A harpooner in the bow, or front, of the whaleboat would plunge his harpoon, which was connected to a long line, into the whale. If the angry, frightened whale tried to swim to safety, the whole boat would be towed along in a terrifying "Nantucket sleigh ride" that could last for hours.

Once the whale was killed by the harpooners—spouting "black blood"—it was towed back to the ship. There, it was tied alongside and whalers would carve its blubber away in huge strips, around and around, like peeling an orange. The strips, called "blankets," were hauled up on deck and cut into smaller pieces that the men could handle more easily. These were cut up into thin sheets called "Bible leaves" and thrown into huge cooking vats on deck called the trypots. In those trypots the blubber was boiled down to get the precious oil. This was called "trying out." The oil was put into barrels—by the hundreds on a successful voyage—that were stored below decks.

In those days, the cleanest, longest-lasting, and brightest candles were made from spermaceti, a white, waxy substance found in a large reservoir in the head of the sperm whale. And whale oil from blubber or spermaceti was the best there was for delicate instruments such as clocks. Whalebone, which is what people called the fringed baleen plates from the mouths of the toothless whales, was also valuable. Before springs and plastic were invented, whalebone had many uses in clothing and anywhere something strong and flexible was needed.

After stowing away the whale oil, the crew would clean every inch of the ship and then wait for the next whale to be spotted, which could take hours, days, weeks, or even months. To pass the time, they told stories of their adventures or carved scrimshaw, which is elaborate decoration of whalebone and whale teeth.

In the second half of the nineteenth century came harpoon guns and whaleships powered by steam engines. These ships were fast enough to catch whales that the sailing ships could not, especially the giant blue whale. Harpoon guns used explosives to fire the dart at the whale, hitting it harder and more often. By the twentieth century, whales were killed so quickly and easily that they were made almost extinct. In one year alone, 1951, the whalers of the world killed 31,000 whales. In 1962, 66,000 whales were killed, the all-time record. By comparison, the New Bedford whalers captured 30,000 whales in 160 years. By the mid-twentieth century, the magnificent blue whale was almost gone, with only about 5,000 left of the 225,000 thought to exist at one time.

Today, whaling is practiced by very few nations, including Japan and Norway, as well as some Native American tribes. Some kinds of whales have increased their populations, such as the sperm whale. Others, like the blue, remain very rare. Today, most of the world realizes how close mankind came to wiping out the whales and is working to protect those that remain and rebuild their numbers.

ABOUT THE WHALEMEN

Herman Melville colorfully described the Quaker captains and owners of whaleships like the *Pequod*. Highly religious and very demanding as employers, they, along with their families, were very important people in New England whaling towns such as New Bedford, and they built fine houses with the money they obtained from their ships' whaling voyages.

Melville also described the crew members of the ships, who were very different from the Quakers—and different from one another. In *Moby Dick*, Tashtego is a Wampanoag Indian from the island of Martha's Vineyard, and Daggoo is a black African. Many men such as these went whaling, and they were joined by others. Farmers from northern New England went to New Bed-

ford and Nantucket to sign aboard whaleships, which tells us something about what a hard life farming had been. Adventure-seeking men from around the world joined whaling crews to seek their fortunes and possibly escape an even harder life.

When whaleships began to make long voyages, they would hire crew members wherever they went—the Azores, Madeira, and Cape Verde Islands in the Atlantic, Hawaii and Fiji in the Pacific. The new people were often necessary because life aboard a whaleship could be awful, with cramped quarters and food that we today would regard as inedible. When men such as Herman Melville jumped ship because of the horrible conditions, they would be replaced by men from wherever the ship happened to be. Sometimes men were even taken aboard ship to be crew members against their will. And although for some officers and crew members whaling could be profitable, some historians regard the working conditions aboard whaleships as something approaching slavery for most of the crew.

In *Moby Dick*, one chapter describes crewmen from Ireland, Iceland, France, Malta, the Isle of Man, Sicily, China, Tahiti, Nantucket, Portugal, England, Spain, and Denmark, all together on the forecastle of the ship, in lively conversation. One can scarcely imagine what the language must have sounded like.

Today, countries around the world look back to the epic whaling voyages of the eighteenth and nineteenth centuries and see how the whalers and their adventures introduced one culture to another. The world-traveling whalers brought the people of Alaska, Japan, and the South Seas together with the people of Europe and North America, connections that are celebrated today with memorials, museums, and cultural exchanges among the descendants of those seafaring adventurers.

A NOTE ABOUT NEW BEDFORD

This retelling of *Moby Dick* was first published by the city of New Bedford, Massachusetts, in 2001, the one hundred and fiftieth anniversary of the publication of Herman Melville's classic novel. As part of the yearlong celebration, the book was created to introduce Melville and *Moby Dick* to students in the city's elementary schools. Now, in this edition, young people everywhere can share in New Bedford's—and America's—whaling heritage.

New Bedford, from which Herman Melville shipped out aboard the whaleship *Acushnet* in 1841, earned its nickname as the Whaling Capital of the World in the mid-1800s. The profits from its vast fleet of whaleships made it the wealthiest city of its size in America, and its name was known everywhere as the whalers circumnavigated the globe.

New Bedford today is full of reminders of the long-departed whaling era. The homes of the whaling captains still line the streets, which are made of the same Belgian paving stones on which horses once pulled carts bearing casks of precious whale oil. Business is conducted in the same buildings where the bankers, tradesmen, ship owners, and craftsmen ran the whaling industry.

On the lawn of the city library stands the famous Whalemen's Statue bearing the prophetic line from *Moby Dick:* "A dead whale or a stove boat." The statue's representation of a harpooner poised at the bow of a whaleboat shows the courage and strength it took to be a whaler. Another testament to the city's whaling history is the New Bedford Whaling Museum. The museum, on Johnnycake Hill, is home to the *Lagoda*, an eighty-nine-foot half-scale replica of a whaling bark—the big-gest ship model in existence. Owned and operated by the Old Dartmouth Historial Society, the Whaling Museum has an unsurpassed collection of whaling artifacts, maritime art, and scholarly research materials. Across the street from the museum stands the Seamen's Bethel. This is the very whalers' chapel described in *Moby Dick*, where Melville himself worshipped before his own whaling voyage.

New Bedford is also the site of the New Bedford Whaling National Historical Park, created by an act of Congress in 1996. The National Park Service has joined local preservationists and historians in working to restore and interpret all the historically important buildings and other materials within the cobblestoned park district and waterfront.

New Bedford, though, is not just about the past. Although the whaling days are long gone, the city remains one of the most important fishing ports in North America and an important destination for marine scientists. It is still known everywhere as the Whaling Capital of the World, as it has been for a century and a half, and its destiny will always be shaped by its historic harbor and its connection to the sea, immortalized in *Moby Dick*.